Contents

Postman Pat and the
Christmas Puddings

by John Cunliffe
illustrated by Joan Hickson

It was a bright day in November. At the post office, Mrs Goggins said, "Ted left a message from Granny Dryden. She's run out of sugar, and she says would you take a two-pound bag when you call."

"Certainly," said Pat. "I hope she's baking something nice."
Mrs Goggins gave Pat a bag of sugar with the letters, and off he went.

Pat called at Greendale Farm with two letters and a parcel. But Mrs Pottage was busy. She was very busy. She said, "Put them on the dresser, Pat. We're too busy to open them just now." The cooker was on. Pans boiled on the hob. The scales were out. The recipe book was open. The table was full. There were bags of flour, and sugar, and raisins, and currants. There were packets of dates, and peel, and ground almonds.

There was a bowl of butter warming by the stove. There was a bowl of brown eggs. There was a small bottle of brandy. Katy and Tom were helping. They weighed the flour. They beat the eggs. They held big wooden spoons, and stirred round and round in the big mixing bowls.

"My goodness," said Pat, "that smells good. Is it for a party?"

"No, it's for Christmas," said Katy.

"It's our Christmas pud," said Tom.

"Pudding," said Mrs Pottage.

"And cake," said Katy.

"Lovely," said Pat, as he helped with an extra stir. "But what's that small bowl for?"

"That's your pudding," said Tom.

"Oh, it was a secret," said Katy.

"Never mind," said Pat, "I'll forget it before Christmas comes."

Mrs Pottage put the puddings on to boil. Tom scraped a bowl. Katy licked a wooden spoon. She gave Pat the other one. They gave baby Paul a bowl to scrape, but he put it on his head!

7

Pat went on his way.

"Now, Jess," he said, "don't let me forget Granny Dryden's sugar." Pat called next on the Reverend Timms. The Reverend was in the kitchen, too, with lots of pans boiling and steaming.

"Are you busy with Christmas puddings as well?" said Pat.

"Bless you, no," said the Reverend. "Miss Hubbard always makes me a lovely one. I could never eat two. No, I'm making grapefruit marmalade. Always comes in handy for church events, you know. Do have a jar for Christmas. It goes nicely on toast."

"Thank you very much," said Pat.

Pat was on his way.
At Thompson Ground, Alf was busy icing the Christmas cake.
"He does it better than me," said Dorothy.

Dorothy had already made the puddings, and she had two ready for Pat.

"Thank you," said Pat, as he went on his way.

"We'll have a lot of puddings by the time Christmas comes," said Pat to Jess, as they went along. "More than we can eat."
Jess would rather have fish any day, so he wasn't bothered.

Granny Dryden was always glad to see Pat, but she was specially glad to see him today.

"Did you bring the sugar?" was the first thing she said.

"Yes, I've brought it," said Pat. "It's been cakes and puddings all the way. It would have been hard to forget."

"Oh, that's lovely," said Granny Dryden. "You are a dear. I'll make you an extra pudding as a special 'thank you'."

"That's er ... very kind of you," said Pat, wondering how many puddings that would make.

Even Ted was busy in the kitchen when Pat called. He had a big machine on the table.

It was whizzing and whirring like a cement-mixer. "Whatever is that?" said Pat.

"It's the Doctor's food-mixer," said Ted. "I've been putting a new motor on it. I'm trying it out on my mum's favourite recipe for ..."

"I can guess," said Pat. "Don't tell me... I bet it's for Christmas pudding."

"You're right!" said Ted. "How did you guess?"

"I can see into the future," said Pat.

"There's just one catch," said Ted.

"You see, it's a big mixer, and it only works with large amounts. I think I've mixed enough for about ten Christmas puddings."

"Oh dear," said Pat.

"Anyway, I'll keep three for you. You'll easily manage three, won't you?"

"Well," said Pat, "I can't..."

11

"I know you like Christmas pudding," said Ted, "so don't be shy about having three. They'll be gone in no time."
And Pat didn't have the heart to say "No".

When Pat called on Miss Hubbard he was glad to see that she was busy making blackberry wine. There were no puddings in sight.
When she said, "I've kept a special bottle of Christmas wine for you, Pat," he was really pleased.

But when she opened the cupboard and took out a fat round packet, and said, "And a real home-made pudding to go with it," poor Pat almost fainted.

He said, in a wobbly voice, "Th..thank y...you very much, Miss H-H-Hubbard."

By the end of the week, Pat had collected ten Christmas puddings in the back of his van.

"Oh, Jess," he said, all these puddings! They're just too much for me. I don't think I could eat even one now."

I don't know what would have happened to all those puddings if Pat hadn't had a broken spring on the van. He had to take his van into Pencaster to get it mended.

He did some Christmas shopping while he waited for it. There was a Christmas tree in the market-place. Some people were collecting for homeless families.

Pat put some money in the collecting box, and the man said, "Thanks. That'll be a good help for the Christmas Dinner."

"Did you say Christmas Dinner?" said Pat. "Is that what you're collecting for?"

"It certainly is," said the man.

"Would you like some lovely home-made puddings?" said Pat. "Ten of them?"

"Great!" said the man. "Just what we need. Great! Thanks!"

In the end, Pat put his name down to help with the dinner.

Everyone loved the puddings, and ate them up to the last morsel.

When Christmas was over, and Pat's friends said, " And how was the pudding?" Pat could truly say, "Delicious! Really delicious."
I wonder if he'll get ten next year?

Postman Pat's
Christmas Surprise

by John Cunliffe
illustrated by Joan Hickson

There was a parcel for Granny Dryden on Tuesday morning. It was her new catalogue from Manchester.

"That's good," she said, "I'll be able to start picking some Christmas presents. But, oh dear, everything seems to cost so much these days."

On Friday, Pat called on Granny Dryden again, with the Pencaster Gazette. She was sucking the end of her old ink-pen and looking very puzzled.

"Whatever are you doing?" said Pat.

"It's this Christmas competition," said Granny Dryden, "in my catalogue."

"Hang on," said Pat, "I'll give you a hand if you like. Now, then, what do you have to do? Hm, yes. Look you can put that in there ... and ... that's sixty-five ... and ... oh, dear ..."

It was a very hard competition. There was a cross-word, and a word finder, and puzzle-pictures, and some number-puzzles.

"I'll never finish it," said Granny Dryden.

"You never know what you can do," said Pat, "with a little help from your friends."

"There are some good prizes," said Granny Dryden. "You can pick anything you like from the catalogue. First prize, items up to £2,000 and £2,000 in cash!"

"Good gracious!" said Pat, "We'll have to give it a try."

"You can borrow the catalogue," said Granny Dryden.

"Thanks," said Pat.

When Pat called at Greendale Farm, he showed the picture-puzzle to Katy and Tom.

"Can you name these pop-stars?" he said.

"Easy," said Katy.

"Simple," said Tom. And they named them all before Pat had finished his glass of milk.

When Pat called on the Reverend Timms, he said, "Now, Reverend, you're good at numbers. Would you just have a look at this puzzle? I'm a bit stuck with it."

"The good Lord will guide us," said the Reverend Timms. "Now where did I put that calculator?"

He had the answer before Pat had finished his cup of coffee.

When Pat called on Miss Hubbard, he said, "Could I have a look in that big dictionary of yours, please? There's a word I'm trying to find."

They had found it by the time Pat had finished his glass of rhubarb-cordial.

By the end of the next week, they had answers to all the questions. "It'll catch the afternoon post," said Pat.

One Saturday morning, Pat called at Greendale Farm. The twins were busy writing their letters to Father Christmas.

"What do you want for Christmas, Pat?" said Tom.
"Oh, hmmm… let's see," said Pat. "I'd love a really good pair of binoculars, to do a spot of bird-watching. But there's not much chance of that."

"You'd better write to Father Christmas," said Katy.
"I will," said Pat. "And what are you asking Father Christmas for?"

21

"A radio-controlled car," said Katy.

"A sledge," said Tom.

"There's not much chance of that," said Mrs Pottage. "But you can ask."

Pat called on the Reverend Timms. He said, "What would you like for Christmas, Reverend?"

"Well," said the Reverend Timms, "I would like a new television. But there's not much chance of that."

"You'd better write to Father Christmas," said Pat.

"I will," said the Reverend Timms.

Pat called on Dorothy Thompson. He said, "What would you like for Christmas, Dorothy?"

"Well, I'd love a good warm pair of slippers," said Dorothy. "And a pair for Alf as well."

"You'd better write to Father Christmas," said Pat.

"I will," said Dorothy.

Pat called on Granny Dryden. He said. "What would you like for Christmas?"

"Oh, there's a lovely warm coat in the catalogue," said Granny Dryden. "It would be just the thing to keep me warm in church. But there's not much chance of that."

"You'd better write to Father Christmas," said Pat.

"I will," said Granny Dryden.

Pat called on Ted Glen. He said, "What would you like for Christmas, Ted?"

"I need a new power-drill," said Ted. "But there's not much chance of that."

"You'd better write to Father Christmas," said Pat.

"I will," said Ted.

Pat called on Miss Hubbard. He said, "What would you like for Christmas, Miss Hubbard?"

"A new bike," said Miss Hubbard, "but there's not much chance of that."

"You'd better write to Father Christmas," said Pat.

"I will," said Miss Hubbard.

The next day Pat called on Granny Dryden he had a good look at her catalogue.

"All the things our friends would like for Christmas," said Pat, "are in your catalogue."

"Let me guess," said Granny Dryden, and she picked a present for each one. She got most of them right first time.

"Well, I don't know if they'll get what they want," she said.

"You never know your luck," said Pat.

They had forgotten all about the competition.

24

Then, there was a very special looking envelope in the post for Granny Dryden.

She was busy making a cake, so she just said, "Pop it behind the clock, Pat. I'll open it when I have time."

"Oh, but it looks important," said Pat, "Wouldn't you like to open it now?"

He just could not wait to see what was in it. But Granny Dryden only said, "Oh, no, I can't be bothered with it. I must get this cake in the oven."

So Pat didn't find out what was in it; not, anyway, until Friday morning. When Pat opened that garden gate, Granny Dryden's door flew open, and she ran down the garden path to meet him. Then she put her arms around Pat and gave him a big hug and a loud kiss. What a surprise Pat had. She had never done such a thing before. He said, "Oh....... Granny Dryden.. goodness me... well...I ...I ...oh...whatever...?"

"Oh, Pat, we've won!" sang Granny Dryden. "We've won! We've won!"

"What?" said Pat.

"The competition! We've won the competition! First prize! Come in and have a cup of tea, and I'll tell you all about it. It was that special letter. I forgot all about it. Then I saw it this morning, when I was dusting."

"Well I never," said Pat, "how much have you won?"

"How much have *we* won," said Granny Dryden, "I could never have done it without you."

"But the Reverend helped with the number-puzzles," said Pat. "And then Miss Hubbard helped with the word-search, and the twins with the pop-stars, and..."

"There'll be a share for everyone," said Granny Dryden, "because we've won the first prize. Remember? £2,000 in cash and £2,000 in things from the catalogue. Oh, Pat, I've had such a good idea. We can make all our friends' Christmas wishes come true. We can pick presents from the catalogue for them."

"I'll be busy when all the parcels come," said Pat.

"And we'll share out the money," said Granny Dryden, "There'll be some for the church fund, and Save the Children Fund, and some to put by for a rainy day."

"Great!" said Pat.

Christmas came at last. There was a big party for everyone in the barn at Greendale Farm. Sam was most puzzled when Pat asked if he could borrow his van for half-an-hour.

In the middle of the party, Pat arrived in Sam's van, flung open the doors, and called out, "Special delivery, everyone!"

And there was the van, full of the most exciting looking parcels. There was one for everyone, and a lucky-dip for the children.

What a time they had! Tom went out into the snow to try out his sledge. Pat spotted a hawk through his binoculars. Granny Dryden was lovely and warm in her new coat. Katy's model car was whizzing about under the tables of food. Ted helped the Reverend to tune his new television. Miss Hubbard had a ride round the duck-pond on her new bike.

When they all had their Christmas dinner, the Reverend Timms lifted his glass and made a speech.

"A big THANKYOU to Granny Dryden and Pat," he said, "for this wonderful party and for all their marvellous presents."

"Oh, but you all helped," said Granny Dryden.
They waved their glasses and gave three cheers.
"This is a Christmas we will never forget," said Pat. "Never!"

Postman Pat's
Christmas Tree

by John Cunliffe
illustrated by Joan Hickson

It was cold and snowy in Greendale. Christmas was coming. Pat had more and more letters and parcels to deliver each day. All the people of Greendale were busy, getting ready for Christmas.

When Pat called at Greendale Farm, Mrs Pottage was making mince-pies.

"Have some mince-pies," said Mrs Pottage.

"Just one, please," said Pat. "I don't want to get fat."

At the school, the children were making streamers and calendars.

"Where is Lucy?" said Pat.
"Poor little Lucy," said Mr Pringle. "She slipped on the ice and broke her leg, last night. She's in Pencaster hospital."
"Oh, dear," said Pat, "that's unlucky, at Christmas. She'll be missing some of the fun. I'll pop over and see her when I've finished my round. See if I can cheer her up."

The children gave Pat a big card and a present to take for Lucy.

Lucy was delighted to see Pat. He told her all the Greendale news, and made her laugh with his jokes. Then he went round the ward to have a chat with the other children.

"Dear me," said Pat to the nurse, "they haven't got many books and toys, have they? It must get a bit dull for them."
"We just haven't got the money for books and toys," said the nurse. "I wish we had."
"We'll have to see what we can do," said Pat.

All the way home, Pat was thinking of ways to raise money for the children at the hospital. And as he went on his round the next day, he asked the people of Greendale.

"We could have a special collection in the church," said the Reverend Timms.

"I'll make some cakes for the Christmas Bazaar," said Dorothy Thompson.

"We could have a raffle," said Miss Hubbard. "I'll give three bottles of my best rhubarb wine." Everyone wanted to help.

On Wednesday the wind got up, and that helped more than anything else, as you will see. It blew a big fir tree into the road, not far from Greendale Farm. Pat couldn't get past with his van, so he went to Peter Fogg, with his tractor and power-saw.

Peter was just going to cut the tree up and drag the pieces away, when Pat had an idea.

"Hang on, Peter," said Pat, "do you think we could move that tree all in one piece?"

"We could with the big tractor," said Peter, "but it'll be a lot easier to cut it up."

"No, don't do that," said Pat, "that tree's given me an idea. It's a Christmas-tree! We could put it up on the village green and get Ted to rig some lights up. Then we could have a special carol concert, and a Christmas Fair in the village hall. Lots of people would come from the towns to see it, and we'd raise plenty of money for the hospital."

They had a real old time moving that tree to the village green. It took two tractors and a trailer in the end. A lot of people came to help, and PC Selby diverted the traffic.

Colonel Forbes brought a huge tub to put the tree in. Ted borrowed a JCB to lift the tree into place. The tree looked lovely, but there was still a lot to do.

The children at the school made decorations to go on the tree, and posters to advertise the carol concert and Greendale Christmas Fair. Ted began fixing up the lights. Then he said, "Why don't we have lights on the church, and the post-office, and the village hall, as well?" And he went off to Pencaster to borrow more lights.

"It's going to be better than Blackpool Illuminations," said Pat.
"We mustn't get carried away," said Miss Hubbard.

Everyone began making extra cakes, and mince-pies, and
Christmas puddings, to sell at the Christmas Fair.

Granny Dryden's knitting needles were going at top speed, making tea-cosies and dishcloths.

Miss Hubbard made a special flower display in the church. It was lovely. There had never been such a busy Christmas in Greendale. Ted arranged special bus trips to Greendale, from Pencaster and Carlisle.

The Pencaster Gazette had a big article on the front page, with a picture of Ted putting the lights up, then they put in free advertisements for three weeks. There was even an article in a colour magazine, on Sunday, with a whole series of photographs, headed:

GREENDALE PREPARES FOR A SPECIAL CHRISTMAS

"We'll have to have a celebrity, to switch the lights on," said Mrs Goggins.

"We have our own celebrity," said Mrs Pottage. "Everyone knows Pat. He'll have to do it. It was all his idea, after all." Everyone agreed with that.

The Big Day was a week before Christmas. Lancaster Silver Band came to play for the carols. The Mayor of Pencaster came to switch the lights on. And crowds of people came. There was even a special train from London. Miss Hubbard had to make several extra trips with the Greendale bus to collect everyone. Radio Pencaster came with their radio car, to report live from the scene.

All was ready. The Mayor made a speech.
"Keep it short," whispered Ted. "It's too cold to hang about."

The moment came to switch the lights on. Pat stepped forward, and pressed the big switch. There was a loud bang, and a splutter, a flash, and a cloud of smoke. The lights flashed on for a moment, then went out. The crowd said:

"Ooooh!"

Then: "Aaaaaaah!"

It was a good thing Ted had his tool-kit handy.

"It's blown a fuse," he said. "Don't worry, I'll soon fettle it."

And he did. The lights came on. The band played. The choir sang.

The crowds joined in. They filled the church for the service. They filled the village hall for the Christmas Fair.

They filled the collecting-boxes for the hospital. It was wonderful. A Christmas to remember for years and years afterwards.

When all the money was collected and counted, there was more than enough to fill the children's ward with books and toys. The rest was given to the hospital funds. After that, children had a much nicer time in hospital, thanks to the tree that blew down, and Pat's bright idea, and all the people of Greendale who joined in to help.

Postman Pat and
the Christmas Post

by John Cunliffe
illustrated by Celia Berridge

It was nearly Christmas and there was deep snow in Greendale. Each day, Pat had more and more Christmas parcels and letters to deliver. Jess had to curl up small to make room for them.

"I've never known such a busy Christmas," said Pat.

Everyone in Greendale was busy getting ready for Christmas. Granny Dryden was busy knitting warm woolly jumpers for all her friends and relations. Ted Glen was busy making wooden trucks and trains.

Alf Thompson was busy making walking-sticks from sheep's horn. Miss Hubbard was busy making beetroot wine, and table-mats, and calendars. Mrs Pottage was busy making poker-work pictures. The Reverend Timms was busy making framed pictures of Greendale Church. Katy and Tom were busy making all kinds of pictures and presents and decorations, at home and at school.

Everyone was busy writing Christmas cards.

And when all these cards and presents had been addressed, and wrapped up, and tied up, and stuck together with sticky-tape, they had to go in the post. When Pat emptied the letter-boxes, they were full to bursting.

Every day, the post-office was full of people, buying stamps, and cards, and string, and sticky-tape, and wrapping-paper, and envelopes; weighing their parcels, and asking for more stamps, and air-mail labels; asking how much it would be to send a parcel to France, or America, or Africa. Poor Mrs Goggins was run off her feet.

"I'm glad Christmas is only once a year," she said.

Then, one cold and frosty morning, Pat had a surprise when he walked into the post-office. Mrs Goggins was smiling.

"I have a helper, now," she said.

"Who can it be?" said Pat.

He could hear someone in the back room, busy sorting the parcels, and singing to himself. "I'm sure I know that voice," said Pat, "but I just can't place it."

"You'll never guess," said Mrs Goggins. "Have a look, and see."

"Well, I never!" said Pat.

It was Ted Glen. He was wearing a special post-office badge, to show that he was a proper post-office Christmas post worker.

"Hello, Pat," said Ted. "How am I doing?"

"You look to be doing a good job, as far as I can see," said Pat.

"I'll give you a hand with the village post," said Ted, "so you can get on with the farms. You'd better get round to them before this snow gets too deep."

"Thanks, Ted," said Pat. "I'll be glad of some help."

Ted set out with a big bag of letters and parcels for the houses of the village.

"One thing," he said, "it gets lighter as you go along. Cheerio!"
Ted was on his way, and Pat soon followed with a van full of Christmas post.

There was a wonderful welcome at each house and farm that Pat called at. They had hot drinks and mince pies ready for him, and presents wrapped in shiny paper, with labels saying, "NOT TO BE OPENED UNTIL 25TH DECEMBER". There were saucers of cream and toy mice for Jess.
"We'll be too full to eat our dinner," said Pat.

The snow went on falling, day after day. Pat was going up the hill to Thompson Ground when his front wheels slipped on the ice, and the whole van skated across the road and into a deep ditch. Now Pat was well and truly stuck.

"What are we going to do now, Jess?" he said. "If we don't get round with these parcels, half the people of Greendale won't get their Christmas presents in time. It's going to be cold waiting for help, too. We'll just have to lock up and walk up the hill to see if Alf can bring his tractor down to pull us out."

Just as Pat was setting out on the long walk, there was the sound of another engine coming up the hill. It was Sam, in his mobile shop. He stopped when he saw Pat's van. It wasn't Sam's usual day for visiting Greendale, so Pat was surprised to see him.

"Hello," said Pat, "what are you doing up this way today?"
"It's a special trip," said Sam. "Look in my van and you'll see why."
"Good gracious!" said Pat. Sam's van had none of its usual groceries in it. He had taken the shelves out, and there was a pile of parcels instead.

"I have a post-office badge, like Ted's," said Sam. "I've hired my van to the post-office, to help with the Christmas post. And it looks as though you're stuck, with a load of parcels still to deliver."

"Yes," said Pat, "and it's getting late. It'll be dark soon, and this snow's getting bad."

"I'll take a share of your parcels," said Sam. "You stay here, and I'll go back and ask Peter Fogg to bring the big tractor to pull you out. He'll be here in a jiffy."

"Thanks," said Pat. "What a good thing you came along."

They shared the parcels out, and Sam went back down the hill. Pat and Jess didn't have long to wait. They were very glad to hear the roar of Peter's engine coming up the hill. Peter soon pulled Pat's van out of the ditch. Then he did better than that. He had his snow-plough fitted to the front of the tractor, so he drove in front of Pat, clearing a way through the snow. Alf and Dorothy Thompson were delighted to see them. They thought they were snowed-in for the week.

"If you hadn't come," said Alf, "we'd have had no parcels, no cards, and no visitors, all Christmas. Bless you, both."

Pat and Peter couldn't stop; they had to push on before snow and darkness stopped them. Peter went ahead, up all the hill roads, and cleared the snow. Pat followed as fast he could, with the post.

When, at last, they got back to the village, and the safety and shelter of the valley, they were cold and tired. Mrs Goggins had hot drinks and Christmas cake waiting for them in her sitting-room behind the post-office, and they sat in front of a big fire to warm their toes. Sam and Ted soon came to join them. Ted's post-bag was empty, and so was Sam's van, but there was a load of parcels for Sam to take to Pencaster to catch the evening post and the train to London.

"Oh, Pat," said Mrs Goggins, "I musn't forget to tell you; there was a phone call from the vicarage. The Reverend said would you please be sure to call at the village hall on your way home tonight. Now you won't forget will you? He said it was important."

"I'll not forget," said Pat.

It was time for everyone to go their different ways. They wished each other "Safe journey!" and "Merry Christmas!" and they were all on their way.

Pat remembered to call at the village hall. And what a scene he saw there! He walked into the middle of the village-institute Christmas party for all the Greendale children. And, who do you think was sitting by the Christmas Tree, giving out presents to the children? Father Christmas himself! Pat said he wished he could have a flying-sleigh, drawn by reindeer, to deliver his parcels, and that made Father Christmas laugh. He had a special present for Jess; a small parcel, done up in a blue ribbon.

"I wonder what it can be," said Pat. "Now Jess will have a parcel to open on Christmas Day."

Pat joined in a dance with the children, and kissed Miss Hubbard under the mistletoe. Jess gave Lucy Selby a kiss; a lick on the nose. Then it was time for Pat to be on his way home.

Christmas Eve soon came. It was time to put out the post-office lights and lock up for the holiday. Mrs Goggins was looking forward to a good rest after all the extra work. Everyone was!

All the cards and parcels had been delivered, and everything was ready for the excitements of Christmas Day itself. The children of Greendale could think of nothing but the moment when Father Christmas would call. Of wakening up very early in the morning, to find a stocking filled with presents at the foot of the bed. Of sitting round the Christmas tree, with a pile of exciting parcels waiting to be opened. Oh, how would the minutes between now and then ever pass?

But they did pass. Very early in the morning, on Christmas Day, lights began to wink on in cottages and farms, wherever children lived, the whole length of Greendale. In Pat's house, young Julian woke Pat and Sara by jumping on their bed with his loaded stocking. He snuggled in between them, to pull his presents out one by one. Then it was out of bed and down to the tree, to see the parcels waiting there. Pat was far too sleepy to open his presents, until he had made a cup of tea. As for Jess, when he saw that it was still dark, he curled up in his basket and went back to sleep.

They had a lovely Christmas, and Pat had three whole days with no letters or parcels to deliver. They went to church for the Reverend Timms' Christmas Day service. Miss Hubbard conducted the choir, who sang beautifully, and Peter Fogg pumped the organ. On Boxing Day, they went to the pantomime in the village hall; it was "Jack and the Beanstalk" this year. On the day after Boxing Day, Jess decided to open his present. He tore it open with his claws, when no one was looking. Then he carried it off in his mouth and hid it somewhere. I wonder what it was?

Snowman Postman

By John Cunliffe
illustrated by Celia Berridge

In the middle of January it became still colder in Greendale. More snow fell. It began to melt; there was some rain; then it froze again. It froze so hard that everything had a coat of ice. When Pat got up in the morning, he could not open the door of his van.

He chipped at the ice with a kitchen-knife, but he still couldn't get his key into the lock. He poured warm water over the lock and over the windows; it still wouldn't open. He held a candle so that its flame licked round the lock. Now the key would go in, but it wouldn't turn. He warmed his key on the stove in the kitchen, until it was nearly too hot to hold. Then, it turned in the lock and opened the door.

Pat was on his way, at last, but, oh, it was so cold! Jess fluffed his fur up, and Pat wore his thickest scarf and gloves.

On the way, they saw Ted Glen. He was busy chopping wood. He had no gloves and no scarf on! Pat stopped for a chat. "Aren't you cold?" he said.

"Not a bit," said Ted. "There's nothing like a bit of chopping to warm you up."

At Greendale Farm, Peter Fogg was breaking the ice on the trough so that the cows could have a drink.

"I bet they'd rather have a warm cup of tea," said Pat.

"I don't know what their milk would taste like," said Peter, "if we gave them tea to drink."

Katy and Tom came running across the stack-yard.

"You're too late, Pat," said Katy. "Our postman's already here."

"Come and see," said Tom.

They took him round the corner by the barn. There stood a snowman postman.

He had coal-eyes and mouth, a carrot-nose, an old scarf round his neck, and a bag for his letters.

"Poor fellow," said Pat. "He has no hat. He'll get a cold head. He can borrow mine, but only for a minute." He put his hat on the snowman's head. Now he looked much more like a real postman.

The twins filled his bag with snowballs, and Pat made him a snow-parcel. Large flakes of snow began to fall from the sky.

"Here come some more letters," said Pat. "I hope he gets them all delivered. I can't see any addresses on them. Now don't forget to make him a snow-Jess, and a hat as well. I must be on my way, and I'd be too cold without my hat."

"I'm going to make him a snow-van," said Tom.
"No, an ice-van," said Pat. "That's what mine was this morning."
Pat took the letters in to Mrs Pottage, then went on his way.

At Thompson Ground, young Bill was making a giant snowball. He had started with a small one. Then he had rolled it round and round on the grass. It grew bigger and bigger, until it was so big that he couldn't move it. Pat gave him an extra push with it. It rolled down the hill, picking up still more snow, and growing bigger. It hit the wall at the bottom and broke into pieces. There was a glove sticking out of one piece.

"So that's where my glove went to," said Bill. "That was a piece of luck. I thought I was going to get into trouble for losing that."

When Pat had delivered all his letters and parcels, he was glad to get home to his warm fireside. There was soon a good meal on the table, then it was time for Pat, and Sara, and young Julian, to watch their favourite television programmes. Jess curled up by the fire, too, and had a cat nap; but, after the News, Jess woke up, walked slowly across the room, mewed, and scratched at the door.

"He wants to go out," said Sara.

"Nay, Jess," said Pat. "You don't want to go out in this weather, do you?"

But Jess did want to go out. He scratched and scratched at the door until Pat opened it. A cold blast of air blew in.

"Brrrrr," said Pat. "Don't be long, Jess. It's cold enough to freeze your tail off." Jess ran down the garden path, into the darkness.

Where was he going? Perhaps to see if the mice had come out of their holes, in the barn at Greendale Farm? Wherever it was, he meant to get there, snow or no snow.

Julian went off to bed, and Pat read him a chapter from his favourite Moomin book. When Pat came downstairs again, Sara said, "Jess hasn't come back. I've just been out to look, and there's no sign of him in the garden. It's snowing hard, too. I do hope he's all right."

"The wind's getting up as well," said Pat. "There'll be drifts by morning; it could get really deep. But I expect Jess's in someone's barn, hunting mice. If it's too cold to come home, he'll find a warm bit of hay to curl up in for the night."

Jess didn't come home that night. The next day, the snow was very deep, and Pat couldn't get his van out until the snow-plough had been along the road. They were all very worried about Jess; there was still no sign of him.

"I'll look in all the barns as I go on my rounds," said Pat, "and ask if anyone's seen him. Somebody's sure to have spotted him. Everyone knows Jess in Greendale."

The snow was deep everywhere, and the wind had piled it up into deep drifts in the fields. Pat kept asking about Jess, but no one had seen him. He looked in all the barns, but there was no sign of Jess anywhere. When he called at Thompson Ground, Alf was just setting out to look for some of his sheep; they were lost in the snow, and they would soon die if they didn't get some food.

"I wonder if your Jess's under a snowdrift, like my sheep," said Alf.

All the farmers knew how the sheep could make a space under the snow, like a little snow-house, and be quite safe in it, for a time. They would huddle together to keep warm, and the walls of snow would keep the cold wind off them. But they had no food under the snow, so the farmers had to find them quickly.

"I'll come and give you a hand, looking for your sheep," said Pat. "I can't deliver any more letters until the snow-plough gets up here. That top road's sure to be blocked."

"Right," said Alf. "Thanks, Pat. Let's get going, then."

They took one of the farm-dogs, Floss, to help sniff out the sheep. They also took a long thin rod and a spade each. The snow was frozen hard, and they could walk on the top of the drifts, without sinking in. The snow was so deep that you could walk right over the tops of the walls. Up the hillside they went. The icy wind blew, and made their noses and cheeks sting.

When they came to a place where Alf thought the sheep might be they stopped, whilst Floss ran about sniffing and snuffling at the snow, pushing her nose into any hole or crack or cranny, by walls and trees where the sheep might have sheltered. Then Alf and Pat gently pushed their long rods down into the snowdrifts, feeling for the snow-cave the sheep could have made.

They tried four deep drifts in this way, but they had no luck. They were just going to turn back to the farm, when Pat said, "What about the old barn in the bottom meadow? They might have gone there for shelter, then been snowed in."

"There's just a chance," said Alf. "We'll have a look there, then we'll go home for a hot mug of tea. I think we've earned it."

The old barn had no roof; it had blown off one windy day that Pat remembered only too well. They tramped across the snow. They were getting tired and cold. Just one more place to look, then they could go and get warm.

The walls of the old barn were open to the snow and to the wind. The snow had blown in, and piled up inside just as deep as it was outside. Floss sniffed and wagged her tail.

"I think she's smelt something," said Alf, "but it might only be a fox." Floss's tail went faster and faster.

"She's certainly found something," Alf went on. "Let's try the rods."

Alf and Pat carefully pushed their rods into the deep snow. Down and down, as far as they could reach. Pat's rod felt different. One moment, he was pushing the rod through the snow, then it went more easily. Perhaps it had come to a space under the snow. Perhaps it had come to the snow-cave made by the warm bodies of the sheep? "Come and try here," said Pat. "I think I can feel something."

Alf came to try in Pat's place. Yes. Yes. It was the same with Alf's rod.

"I think we've found something," said Alf. "We'd better dig it out, and have a look."

They dug down into the drift. It was hard work, but it made them warm. Floss ran about in the snow, yelping with excitement. Far down, under the snow, in a corner by the wall, Pat uncovered a hole in the snow.

They stopped digging. A woolly nose came to the little gap, and sniffed.

"Thank goodness," said Alf, "we've found them!"

They had to dig more slowly and carefully, now. They didn't want to hurt the sheep with the sharp spades. They made the hole bigger and bigger, until it was big enough to get the sheep out. They could see more woolly bodies cuddled together under the snow, and they could feel how warm they were. The sheep didn't want to come out; it was warmer under the snow than it was out in the cold wind. Alf had to pull them out, one by one.

"There must be about ten of them in there," said Alf.

But Alf and Pat were very surprised when they saw what else was in there with the sheep, keeping warm amongst their woolly coats. There was a small black and white shape there, and it uncurled and ran to Pat when it saw him!

"Jess!" said Pat. "It's my Jess! Dear little Jess, whatever are you doing here, under the snow? Are you all right, Jess?"

He picked Jess up, and tucked him inside his warm overcoat. "Well, I never," he said.

Jess began to purr. He snuggled under Pat's coat, with just his nose peeping out. He soon felt as warm as toast.

"I wonder how you got here, with Alf's sheep?" said Pat. "I wonder."

But Jess couldn't tell him, so Pat never found out.

Pat and Jess went back to the farm to get some bales of hay for the sheep. Pat left Jess by the fire, and Dorothy gave him a saucer of milk. My goodness, how he purred. He almost purred his head off.

Pat and Alf came back to warm themselves by the fire, and have a good hot drink. They felt like purring, too; it was so good to be warm again.

Later, Alf would go with the tractor to bring the sheep back to the farm. As they sat there, they heard something climbing the hill, and going on past the farm, with its diesel engine at full power, and a shwooshing sound going with it.

"That sounds like the snow-plough," said Pat. "I expect Peter Fogg's driving it. That means I can get on with these letters. I'd better be on my way."

"Thanks for helping with the sheep," said Alf.

"Thanks for helping me to find Jess," said Pat. "Cheerio!"

It was a long, cold, journey for Pat that day, round all the frozen farms and cottages. Jess stayed curled up in his warm basket.

When Pat was on his way home, he called in at Greendale Farm, to see how the postman-snowman was getting on. There was no sign of him. He was buried under a huge drift of snow.

"Poor fellow," said Pat. "I hope he has some snow-sheep to keep him warm under there."

Then it was time to go home.

That night, Jess stayed by the fireside. He didn't scratch at the door; not once.